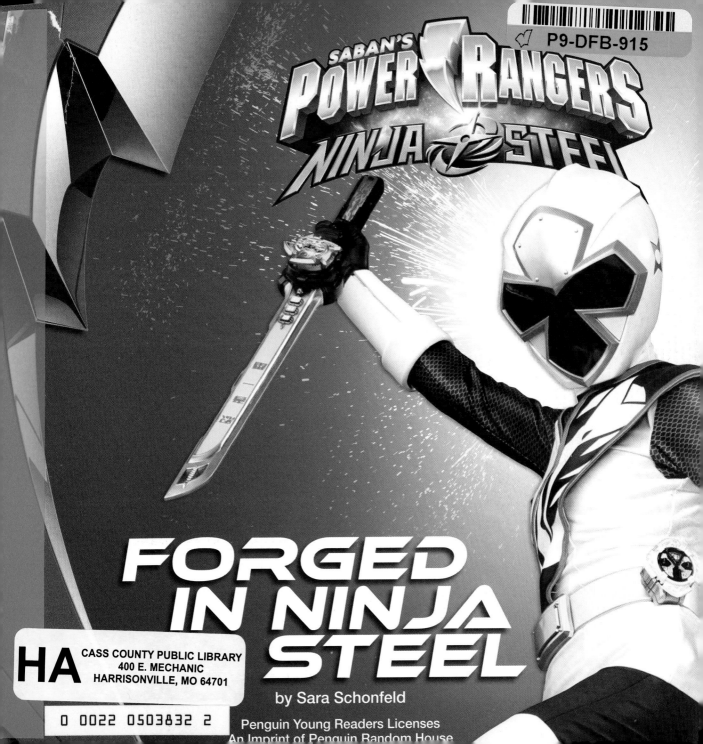

SABAN'S

POWER RANGERS
NINJA STEEL

FORGED IN NINJA STEEL

by Sara Schonfeld

Penguin Young Readers Licenses
An Imprint of Penguin Random House

PENGUIN YOUNG READERS LICENSES
An Imprint of Penguin Random House LLC

ISBN 9780515159738   10 9 8 7 6 5 4 3 2 1

When Galvanax, Champion of *Galaxy Warriors*, stole the Ninja Nexus Star, Earth's greatest ninja sacrificed himself to keep the universe safe. Years later, a new team has risen to protect the Power Stars. Three stars have yet to be pulled from the Ninja Nexus Prism. Who will be chosen next?

Calvin slammed down the hood of his truck.

"Should be all fixed," he said.

Suddenly, big pieces of metal started falling from the sky!

Both Hayley and Calvin got out of the truck to investigate.

"What is this stuff?" Hayley said. "They don't look like parts from an airplane."

"Maybe it's an alien!" Calvin joked. He threw some slime at her.

Calvin picked up a strange-looking rock and suddenly it shape-shifted!

The strange rock was now an even stranger man.

"What are you?" Hayley asked.

"Hi, I'm Mick," the alien said. "I got separated from my friend Brody. He's from Earth!"

He tried to call Brody on his data-com, but it was broken.

"It must have broken when we jumped from the spaceship," Mick said.

"Why would you jump from a spaceship?" Calvin asked.
"We were escaping monsters," Mick said. "Just like those!"
He pointed behind them.

Hayley and Calvin looked at the monsters, and at their new friend Mick.

"Maybe we can scare them off?" Hayley suggested.

They both attacked the monsters. Mick hid in the truck.

The monsters had spears, but Hayley and Calvin fought together.

Finally they could escape! They jumped into the truck and drove away.

Just in time, too—Ripcon appeared.

"You fools!" he said to the monsters. "They got away. But not for long!"

Back on his spaceship, Galvanax was furious.

"For ten years, no monster could pull out the Ninja Power Stars," he roared. "But three human teenagers did it, no problem at all. How? I will destroy all of them!"

And he knew how. He had spent ten years searching the galaxy for the scariest monsters for his television show, *Galaxy Warriors*.

Galvanax ran onto the stage for *Galaxy Warriors* in the Warrior Dome. All the monsters cheered.

"It's time for a new twist to our show," he said. "Any contestant that can destroy the Power Rangers and bring me their Ninja Power Stars becomes a *Galaxy Warriors* Champion, just like me!"

All the monsters yelled. They were ready to fight the Power Rangers!

Meanwhile, on Earth, Hayley and Calvin brought Mick to their shop class, where they built and fixed things.

"There's plenty of tools in this class," Calvin said. "So hopefully we can fix that wrist-thing of yours."

Mick tried to blend in—without transforming into anything.

But their principal spotted him right away!

"You must be our new shop teacher!" Principal Hastings said. "I'm glad you changed your mind. Good luck."

Mick spent all day fixing his data-com.

He wanted to get in touch with his friend Brody. They had both been prisoners of Galvanax, and now they were finally free.

Mick was ready to test his data-com.

"Let's hope it will power up," he said. He pressed a button. The data-com was working!

"Brody? Are you okay?" Mick asked.

"We're in trouble," Brody said. He was with his new friends Sarah and Preston, the other Power Rangers. "We know where the Ninja Steel is, and so does Galvanax. We need to get to the high school. It's in my dad's trophy."

Calvin, Hayley, and Mick raced to the trophy cabinet. They found the trophy with Brody's dad's name on it. The Ninja Steel was inside, just like Brody had said!

But they heard buzzing outside. Buzzcams, spies for Galvanax! That meant one thing—Galvanax had found them. And if Galvanax knew where they were, he would send someone to fight them for the Ninja Steel. A monster must be nearby!

Suddenly a horrible monster appeared. His name was Ripperrat.

He shot energy blasts at the team, and Mick fell over.

Hayley and Calvin grabbed what they could find: a baseball bat and a tennis racket! They attacked Ripperrat.

"I gave you a sporting chance," Ripperrat said. "Now the game's over!"
Calvin looked down. His metal bat was bent like it was clay!
There was no way they could win!
Ripperrat was about to take the Ninja Steel when suddenly the Nexus Prism appeared!
The monster went flying.

Mick, Calvin, and Hayley walked over to the Prism.

"It's the Yellow and White Power Stars," Mick said. "They're glowing. Grab the Power Stars!"

Calvin and Hayley reached in and pulled out the stars, and the Prism shot away into the sky.

"You pulled out the Ninja Power Stars. Do you know what that means?" Mick asked.

"It means you're Power Rangers," Brody said. He ran over with Preston, Sarah, and Redbot.

"Just like us," Sarah said.

But they didn't have long for introductions.

Ripperrat was back!

"I'm going to make you all pay for stealing from Champion Galvanax," he said.

"Just follow my lead," Brody said.
"It's Morphin Time!"
   The team locked their stars into
their Ninja Battle Morphers, and they
morphed into Power Rangers!

All five of them attacked Ripperrat
with their Battle Morphers.
Ripperrat didn't stand a chance!
Ninjas win! Or so they thought.

Back in the Warrior Dome, Galvanax was furious. His monster was destroyed!

"The show's not over yet!" he said. The spaceship sent a beam of energy and Ripperrat was gigantified—he returned, bigger and scarier than ever!

Brody and the rest of the Power Rangers were scared. How could they defeat Ripperrat now? WHOOSH! The Prism reappeared and showed the team a vision of gigantic robots.

"If the legends are true, those are your Zords!" Mick said.

Mick reached into the trophy and pulled out Ninja Throwing Stars. He tossed them into the Prism, and new stars flew into the Rangers' hands.

"I think you're about to meet your Zords," Mick said.

A team of huge robots appeared, one for each Power Ranger!
Preston had a magic blue Zord shaped like a dragon. Sarah had a
speeding pink train—a Zoom Zord! The Nitro Zord, a huge yellow truck,
was Calvin's. And the dog Zord was Hayley's. It looked just like her dog
Kodiak!

"It looks just like Redbot!" Brody said, pointing to his Zord. "I'll call you Robo-Red Zord."

The team used their Zords to attack Ripperrat again.

The whole team had to work together. Preston's Zord used its fire breath, and then the Power Rangers used their Ninja Blasters to finish Ripperrat forever!

Now that Summer Cove was Ripperrat-free, the team returned to school.

"I need to say thanks for saving us today," Brody said. "I'm sorry, getting you all involved—it was all an accident."

"The Prism chose the five of you to be Power Rangers," Mick said.

"So, it's our job to save the earth?" Calvin asked.

"I guess so," Brody said.

"Then let's get to work," Hayley said.

Sarah looked into the Prism.

"Brody," she said, "didn't you say there were six Ninja Power Stars? Because we only pulled out five."

Brody joined her.

"You're right," he said. "The Gold Star is gone. Someone must have pulled it out."

"But who?" Sarah asked.